S0-AYA-558

SOMETHING IS WRONG AT MY HOUSE

A BOOK ABOUT PARENT'S FIGHTING

Written by DIANE DAVIS
Illustrated by MARINA MEGALE

ACKNOWLEDGEMENTS

I would like to extend my gratitude to all of the many caring individuals, both locally and nationwide, whose suggestions and encouragement aided me in writing *Something Is Wrong At My House.*

Special thanks to:

Eastside Domestic Violence Project
Bellevue, Washington
Lee Drechsel, Director
Jean Williams, Children's Therapist

New Beginnings Shelter for Battered Women
Seattle, Washington
Kathy Pruitt, Children's Advocate
Nan Stoops, Volunteer Coordinator

Shari Steelsmith for her fine editing, organizational skills and positive attitude,
Betsy Crary for her wisdom, friendship and careful guidance throughout this project
        and to
Joan Misenar, whose sensitivity, understanding and belief in me, led me back to my writing.

This book is dedicated to my sons, Matthew and Joshua.

Second Printing 1985

INTRODUCTION

The purpose of this book is to help break the generational cycle of domestic violence. The best place to start is with the youngest generation, the children, because they are still forming their ideas and choosing ways to live their lives. *Something Is Wrong At My House* is directed at those children.

The book is based on a true story about a boy living in a violent household. He experiences the universal feelings of fear, anger and hopelessness common to victims of domestic violence although not readily expressed by those of some cultural backgrounds. In the story he is able to acknowledge such feelings and make a decision to look for ways to cope with them. He explores both internal and external ways of coping; he finds ways to care for himself and he seeks help from the outside.

Something Is Wrong At My House helps all children, those from violent and non-violent homes, by giving them permission to have feelings, acknowledge them and make decisions about how they wish to act on them. Children may choose to act out their anger directly or channel it constructively like excelling at school or in sports.

Teachers can read this non-threatening story to their classes as a group and present ways of coping with this serious problem. Counselors can use the book with children and their parents in order to help children identify their feelings and review appropriate alternatives.

The format of this book is designed to permit use with both preschool and school aged children. The longer text on the left was written for the older children; the shorter captions beneath the illustrations are directed toward younger children.

Domestic violence is painful. As children identify their feelings and learn to see their options, they **can** break the cycle of violence.

Something's wrong at my house.

Something at my house is very wrong. My mom and dad have terrible fights. Sometimes there is yelling and shouting. But other times there is pushing, hitting, kicking and even throwing things.

My mommy and daddy have terrible fights.

3

It SCARES me and I don't know what to do. I don't like all the hurting. I see Dad hurting Mom, and I'm afraid that I will get hurt too. I am scared of not knowing what is going to happen next.

I feel all alone. I am ashamed of what keeps happening at our house. I am scared that if I tell someone about it, my parents or I might get into trouble or no one will believe me.

It SCARES me and I don't know what to do. 5

I also feel MIXED UP. Does the fighting start because of me? Is it because my parents don't want me or love me or because **they** have a problem?

I'm not sure what is *right* or *wrong* anymore. No matter what I do or how I act, the fighting still goes on. I wish the fighting would stop.

Do they fight because **they** have a problem?

I get so scared sometimes I have bad dreams.

Being afraid makes me want to run away or hide or *grow up fast* so I can protect myself and my mom and my little sister.

I get so scared sometimes I have bad dreams.

Sometimes I also feel MAD. I feel mad at my dad for being like this. I feel mad at my mom for not finding a way to make things better. I feel mad that I have to grow up in a home like this. Sometimes I'm even mad at the whole world!

I am mad that I have to grow up in a home like this.

When I'm mad I often feel like hitting and being mean. I want to hit my dad back for hurting my mom. I feel like hitting my mom when I want my own way and she says, "No." I pick on my little sister. I kick my dog and tease my cat. Sometimes I lie about where I'm going and what I've been doing.

When I'm mad I pick on my little sister. 13

There are times when I have trouble at school too. When I think about things that are happening at home I sometimes feel like fighting with my friends. I talk back to my teacher. I don't feel like doing my work so I copy other people's answers. Sometimes I even take other people's things.

I don't feel like having fun like the other kids. I get quiet and stay away from people. Sometimes I feel sad and cry a lot.

I wish it didn't have to be like this.

At school I have trouble too.

When I asked Mom why she and Dad fight so much she said, "We are going through a tough time right now, but we will work things out. You are not to blame for our arguments."

I wish we could be a happy family. I want the fighting to stop. I don't want to see all the hurting. I don't want to feel mad, scared, ashamed and mixed up anymore.

I want to feel better.

I wish we could be a happy family.

What can I do?

I can make a list of my feelings or draw pictures about how I feel.

I can get rid of some of the mad feelings in me without hitting or being mean. I feel better when I

run,
dance,
jump rope,
play my drums,
draw a picture,
write a story
or make up a song.

I can get rid of some of the mad feelings in me
without hitting.

And, I can do something that makes me happy. I can:

go to the park,
talk to a friend,
read my favorite book
or cuddle with my cat.

And I can do something that makes me happy.

I can also talk to a grownup, but I'm not sure who will listen.

I could choose my teacher, school counselor, pastor, librarian, babysitter or my best friend's mom, but I'm not sure what to say.

What can I say to them?

I can also talk to a grown-up.

Maybe I can talk to my neighbor...

Chris:	Something is wrong at my house.
Mrs. Brown:	What's wrong?
Chris:	My dad keeps hitting my mom.
Mrs. Brown:	Oh, it can't be that bad. It isn't any of my business anyway.

I guess she didn't believe me. What shall I do now?

I can talk to my neighbor.

I will find someone else who will listen. I can try my teacher..

Chris: Something is wrong at my house. My dad keeps hitting my mom and hurting her. What can I do to make him stop?

Ms. Cortez: Your dad will have to learn ways to solve his problems without hitting. *You* can't make him stop. What you *can* do is take care of yourself. Have you talked to your mom about what is happening at your house?

Chris: Yes, but she just says she and dad are going through a tough time right now and things will get better. They don't get better. They keep getting worse.

Ms. Cortez: Have you talked to anyone else about how you feel?

Chris: Yes, my neighbor, but she said it was none of her business.

Ms. Cortez: I can tell you are upset about this. It is good that you haven't given up on asking for help. I will do some calling to see what more can be done. Stop by tomorrow after school and I will tell you what I have found out.

I can talk to my teacher.

I now know who to call...

My teacher talked to me yesterday. She explained that Domestic Violence happens in all kinds of families but some kids are too scared or too ashamed to tell anyone what is going on.

Ms. Cortez said that I am taking good care of myself by talking about my feelings. She gave me a list of numbers* I can call for help. I can call the numbers myself or have a grown-up call for me. The people at these numbers understand Domestic Violence and will tell me what I should do next.

* State Coalition For Domestic Violence
  Local Shelter For Battered Women
  (call operator for this number if State Coalition cannot be reached)
  Community Crisis Line
  Police
  Child Protective Services

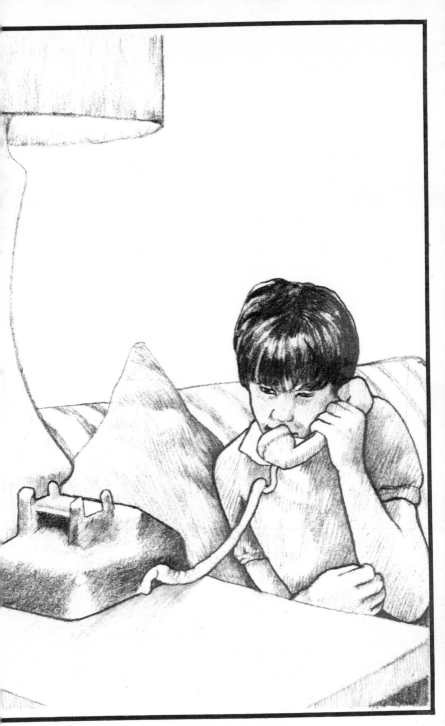

I now know who to call.

There **are** things that I can do myself. I can:

find ways to get out lots of mad feelings without hitting,
do things that make me happy,
talk to a grown-up
and call an agency myself.

I can do things to help myself.

I am a very special, loveable person.
My needs are important;
I deserve to be safe and happy, and so do you.

NATIONAL AND STATE RESOURCES

NATIONAL COALITION AGAINST DOMESTIC VIOLENCE
1500 Massachusetts Ave., NW #35
Washington, DC 20005
202-347-7017

ABAMA COALITION AGAINST
OMESTIC VIOLENCE
eplace, Inc.
. Box 10456   Florence, AL 35631
5-767-3076 (w)

ASKA NETWORK ON DOMESTIC
OLENCE & SEXUAL ASSAULT
0 Seward St., #13   Juneau, AK 99801
7-586-3650

RKANSAS COALITION AGAINST
OLENCE TO WOMEN AND CHILDREN
. Box 807   Harrison, AR 72601
1-741-6167

RIZONA STATE AGAINST DOMESTIC
OLENCE
. Box 27365   Tempe, AZ 85282
2-234-4402

OUTHERN CALIFORNIA COALITION ON
ATTERED WOMEN
O. Box 5036   Santa Monica, CA 90405
3-392-9874

ORTHERN CALIFORNIA SHELTER
JPPORT SERVICES
O. Box 1955   San Mateo, CA 94401
5-342-0850

ENTRAL CALIFORNIA COALITION
N DOMESTIC VIOLENCE
O. Box 3931   Modesto, CA 95352
9-575-7037

OLORADO DOMESTIC VIOLENCE
OALITION
O. Box 18902   Denver, CO 80218
3-394-2810

ONNECTICUT TASK FORCE ON
BUSED WOMEN
O. Box 14299   Hartford, CT 06114
03-524-5890

ISTRICT OF COLUMBIA
y Sister's Place
O. Box 29596   Washington, DC
02-529-5991

LOUISIANA COALITION AGAINST
DOMESTIC VIOLENCE
c/o Crescent House
1231 Prythania   New Orleans, LA 70130
504-523-3755

MAINE COALITION FOR FAMILY CRISIS
SERVICES
P.O. Box 304   Augusta, ME 04861
207-623-3569

MARYLAND NETWORK AGAINST
DOMESTIC VIOLENCE
2427 Maryland Ave.   Baltimore, MD 21218
301-268-4393

MASSACHUSETTS COALITION OF
BATTERED WOMEN'S SERVICE GROUPS
25 West St., 5th Floor   Boston, MA 02111
617-426-8492

MICHIGAN COALITION AGAINST
DOMESTIC VIOLENCE
10435 Lincoln, Huntington Woods, MI 48070
313-547-1051

MINNESOTA COALITION FOR BATTERED
WOMEN
435 Aldine St.   St. Paul, MN 55104
612-646-6177

MISSISSIPPI COALITION AGAINST
DOMESTIC VIOLENCE
P.O. Box 333   Biloxi, MS 39533
601-436-3809

MISSOURI COALITION AGAINST
DOMESTIC VIOLENCE
27 North Newstead   St. Louis, MO 63108
314-781-9948

MONTANA COALITION AGAINST
DOMESTIC VIOLENCE
P.O. Box 6183   Great Falls, MT 59406
406-228-4435

NEBRASKA TASK FORCE ON DOMESTIC
VIOLENCE & SEXUAL ASSAULT
YWCA
222 South 29th St.   Omaha, NE 68131
402-345-6555

NEVADA NETWORK AGAINST DOMESTIC
VIOLENCE
680 Greenbrae Dr., #270 Sparks, NV 89431
702-358-4214

NEW HAMPSHIRE COALITION AGAINST
FAMILY VIOLENCE
P.O. Box 353   Concord, NH 03301
603-224-8893

NEW JERSEY COALITION FOR
BATTERED WOMEN
206 W. State St.   Trenton, NJ 08608
609-695-1758

NEW MEXICO COALITION AGAINST
DOMESTIC VIOLENCE
La Casa, Inc.
P.O. Box 2463   Las Cruces, NM 88004
505-526-6661

NEW YORK STATE COALITION AGAINST
DOMESTIC VIOLENCE
5 Neher St.   Woodstock, NY 12498
914-679-5231

NORTH CAROLINA ASSOCIATION OF
DOMESTIC VIOLENCE PROGRAMS
P.O. Box 595   Wilmington, NC 28402
919-343-0703

NORTH DAKOTA COUNCIL ON ABUSED
WOMEN'S SERVICES
State Networking Office
311 Thayer, Rm 127   Bismarck, ND 58501
701-255-6240

ACTION FOR BATTERED WOMEN IN
OHIO
P.O. Box 2421   Youngstown, OH 44509
216-793-3363

OKLAHOMA COALITION ON DOMESTIC
VIOLENCE & SEXUAL ASSAULT
124 Colorado   Woodward, OK 73801
405-256-8712

OREGON COALITION AGAINST
DOMESTIC VIOLENCE & SEXUAL
ASSAULT
2336 SE Belmont St.   Portland, OR 97214
503-239-4486

PENNSYLVANIA COALITION AGAINST
DOMESTIC VIOLENCE
2250 Elmerton Ave.   Harrisburg, PA 17110
717-652-9571 or 1-800-932-4632

RHODE ISLAND COUNCIL ON DOMEST
VIOLENCE
P.O. Box 1829   Providence, RI 02912
401-272-9524

SOUTH CAROLINA COALITION AGAINS
DOMESTIC VIOLENCE & SEXUAL ASSAU
P.O. Box 7291   Columbia, SC 29202

SOUTH DAKOTA COALITION AGAINST
VIOLENCE
Resource Center for Women
317 S. Kline   Aberdeen, SD 57401
605-226-1212

TENNESSEE COALITION AGAINST
DOMESTIC VIOLENCE
P.O. Box 831   Newport, TN 37821
615-623-3125

TEXAS COUNCIL ON FAMILY VIOLENC
509-A West Lynn   Austin, TX 78746
512-482-8200

UTAH DOMESTIC VIOLENCE COUNCIL
C/o Division of Family Services
150 West North Temple,Salt Lake City 8410

VERMONT:
Chris Phelps   c/o Herstory House
P.O. Box 313   Rutland, VT 05701
802-775-3232 or 802-775-6788

VIRGINIANS AGAINST DOMESTIC
VIOLENCE
P.O. Box 5602   Richmond, VA 23220
804-780-3505

WASHINGTON STATE SHELTER
NETWORK
1063 S. Capital Way #217
Olympia, WA 98501
206-753-4621
Statewide Hotline   800-562-6025

WEST VIRGINIA COALITION AGAINST
DOMESTIC VIOLENCE
P.O. Box 2463   Elkins, WV 26241
304-636-3232

WISCONSIN COALITION AGAINST
WOMAN ABUSE
953 Jennifer St.   Madison, WI 53703
608-255-0539

WYOMING COALITION ON FAMILY
VIOLENCE & SEXUAL ASSAULT
P.O. Box 1127   Riverton, WY 82501

PARENTING PRESS, INC.

Presents

PROTECT YOUR CHILD FROM SEXUAL ABUSE

by Janie Hart-Rossi

This parents guide includes *facts* you need to know about sexual abuse, *key phrases* children can use to resist uncomfortable touch, and *specific activities* you can do with children to reduce the likelihood of their being molested. Designed to accompany *It's MY Body*, by Lory Freeman.

64 pages, 5½ x 8½　　　　　$5.00 paperback

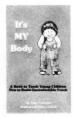

IT'S MY BODY

by Lory Freeman

This children's book can be used alone or in conjunction with *A Parents' Resource Guide*. It offers children a strategy for dealing with uncomfortable touch whether it is tickling or more serious abuse.

24 pages, 5½ x 8½　　　　　$3.00 paperback

WITHOUT SPANKING OR SPOILING

A PRACTICAL APPROACH TO TODDLER AND PRESCHOOL GUIDANCE
by Elizabeth Crary

This book includes lots of ideas to reduce child-parent conflicts without resorting to physical violence. It is easy to understand, easy to use and appropriate for use with young children.

102 pages, 8½ x 11　　　　　$7.95 paperback

DATE DUE

MAR 21 2013	

ng at